Chat
et
Chat Mollo

D'abord, on joue !

Relie les lettres de l'alphabet dans l'ordre.

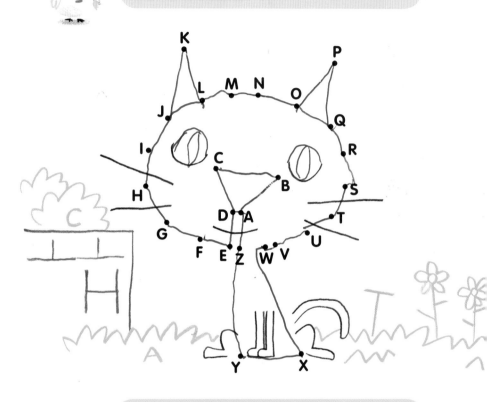

Le mot « **chat** » est caché dans l'image, le vois-tu ? Trouve les lettres !

Super !

Aide Chat Molli à lire ces mots qui font « ch ».

chat   atchoum   chanter

chocolat   chouette   chatouille

chaud   chalet   Chamallows

 chanson   chameau   chausson

Que fait Chat Mollo ?

Chouette ! Chat Mollo…

… mange un Chamallows ?

… chausse ses chaussons ?

… chante une chanson ?

3

Bravo !

Maintenant, on se détend la langue !

la la la li la lo lu li lou

Qui fait quoi ?

Relie les phrases aux dessins.

 aime voler haut.

 aime rouler vite.

 pédale dur !

 aime voguer sur l'eau.

Chat Molli et Chat Mollo sont dans un bateau.

Qui rame? Qui tombe à l'eau?

Sauras-tu découvrir le titre de cette histoire?

Retourne le livre pour lire la réponse.

Un peu de **gym**!

cha che chi cho chu chou

Quelle histoire!

 est tout petit.

 est ramollo.

 fait du

 aime les

Chat Molli et Chat Mollo
sont de grands amis!

En route pour l'aventure!

Et maintenant, ton histoire !

Chat Molli
et
Chat Mollo

Une histoire d'Agnès Cathala,
illustrée par Laurent Richard.

Voici Molli. Voici Mollo.
Molli aime les fruits.
Mollo aime les Chamallows.

Le plus petit, c'est Molli.
Le plus gros, c'est Mollo.

8

Molli est **sportif**, jamais ramolli.
Mollo est **pensif**, toujours ramollo.
Qui bouge pour deux ? Molli.
Qui mange pour trois ? Mollo.

Et les deux meilleurs amis,
c'est Mollo et Molli !

Quand Chat Molli et Chat Mollo
sont dans un bateau,

Chat Molli rame sur les flots et
Chat Mollo mange des gâteaux.

Quand Chat Molli et Chat Mollo
sont dans une auto,

Chat Molli conduit et Chat Mollo
fait dodo.

Quand Chat Molli
et Chat Mollo
sont sur un vélo,

Chat Molli a les pieds
sur les pédales
et Chat Mollo a la tête
dans les étoiles.

Quand Chat Molli
et Chat Mollo
sont à la plage,

Chat Molli fait des châteaux
et Chat Mollo travaille...
son **bronzage** !

13

Quand Chat Molli et Chat Mollo
sont dans un hélico...
Quoi? Chat Mollo dans un hélico?
Mais non! Chat Mollo reste en bas
et Chat Molli vole haut.

Quand Chat Molli et Chat Mollo
sont au supermarché,

Chat Molli pousse le chariot
et Chat Mollo le remplit.

Et quand Chat Molli et Chat Mollo
sont dans la cuisine,

Chat Molli met la table
et Chat Mollo met sa serviette!

La nuit, quand Chat Mollo
et Chat Molli font dodo,
qui tombe du lit?

C'est Chat Molli!

En plein dodo, le gros
met le petit K.-O.
Le champion du dodo,
c'est Chat Mollo, bravo!

Fin

Tu as aimé?

Oui?

Chouette alors!

Allez, maintenant, on se détend!

Tourne la page...

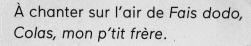

Comptine

À chanter sur l'air de *Fais dodo, Colas, mon p'tit frère.*

Fais dodo, Molli, mon p'tit chat,
Fais dodo, Mollo n'y est pas...
Mollo est en bas
Qui prend un repas.
Molli est en haut
Qui fait un gros dodo.

Fais dodo, Molli, mon p'tit chat,
Fais dodo, Mollo n'y est pas...

23

À bientôt !

© 2015 Éditions Milan
300, rue Léon-Joulin, 31101 Toulouse Cedex 9 – France
www.editionsmilan.com
Loi 49.956 du 16.07.1949 sur les publications
destinées à la jeunesse.
Dépôt légal : 1er trimestre 2015
ISBN : 978-2-7459-7256-9
Imprimé en France par Pollina - L70539A

Gypsy's Gift

Robin H. Soprano

Foreword

This small book is packed with large surprises. Intended as a means to show of Robin H. Soprano's fiction work, not only does the material within contain the heart-warming story *Gypsy's Gift*, this book also contains excerpted chapters from each of Robin's current novels, *A Soul Mate's Promise*, *Absinthe*, and the soon to be published *Three Blind Wives*.

Writers today struggle to attain key elements to their success and their ability to gain exposure, garner reviews, develop loyal audiences. What better way to achieve these goals than to offer a small book at a great price to give readers a sample of their work.

All of the material in this book showcases Robin's talent as a rising author. We sincerely hope you enjoy the contents within and that you will be inclined to check out her other books as well.

Lastly, please remember that reviews are crucial to a writer's success. A review takes but a moment. The benefits to the author in contrast are far-reaching. Those few moments where you write a couple lines in review of a book builds a long-term portfolio which helps others discover this new author.

Thank you for reading Gypsy's Gift.

Michael Ray King – Five-time Royal Palm Literary Award-winning author.

Robin H. Soprano

Gypsy's Gift

A memory, one that has been stuck in my head from about fifty-plus years ago, shoots around my mind. I look over at my eldest daughter sitting by my bedside, her eyes tired with puffy bags.

"Sarah," I whisper, still drowsy from another nap, "I have to tell you a story."

Her eyes search mine. "It's okay, Daddy. Tell me later when you're more awake."

"No, there is something I want you to know. I don't know how many more days or hours I have left on this earth, but rest assured, we are not alone. Don't be scared for me. I was given a gift, so to speak, I guess from heaven, or whatever powers that exist. I remembered this happened to my grandfather, too. Everyone thought he was hallucinating."

She looks at me deeper, eyebrow cocked in confusion.

"Daddy, what are you talking about?"

"Gypsy—where is Gypsy?" I ask.

"The dog? Daddy, what do you want the dog for?"

I take a deep breath. "Humor me; I'm old and I'm dying."

Sarah stands from her chair and hesitantly calls for my beloved dog Gypsy. The dog enters my bedroom with still a little pep in her old trot-like gait. My eyes meet hers, a little cloudy but still a nice whiskey-colored amber. Gypsy is a collie mix. Always loyal and smart, she's going on ten years old. She is healthy. I am not. Seems I basically have a rusty ticker. My heart is tired, and a cranky aneurism on a valve could blow any time. Luckily, I'm not in pain and don't need any medication except the pills that keep my blood thin. I'm just so darn tired all the time.

"Okay, Daddy, what is this talk about a gift?"

I summon the dog to get up on the bed as I prop myself up on some pillows. She complies and settles down, facing me. I motion to Sarah to sit back down. She does with a sigh. Gypsy and I glance at Sarah then back at each other, and there it is: a voice. A beautiful voice like an angel in my head, but it's coming from Gypsy.

"She's not going to believe you."

"Before I explain this extraordinary thing, I'm going to tell you about Grandpa Marty."

Sarah curls up on the recliner next to my bed and throws a soft blanket over her legs.

Gypsy lifts her head, and her eyes meet mine again.

"Keep it brief. We all know you tend to ramble."

"I DON'T RAMBLE," I say firmly to Gypsy.

"I didn't say you did, Daddy."

I smile up at my daughter. "Sorry, sweetie. Wasn't talking to you."

Her face looks confused and a little frightened. "What…"

"It's what I'm trying to tell you. Look, just listen and keep an open mind, please," I beg.

"All right, Daddy. Go ahead."

"When I was about fifteen or sixteen, my Grandpa Marty's cancer had spread and he was in pain. His dog, Muzzy, would sit on the bed day and night. We all thought, *Yes, Muzzy knows and he's watching*. Gramps every now and then would try to speak, and most of the time he didn't make sense. He was on heavy-duty narcotics, and he would babble much ado about nothing. He started to tell me and Grandma that Muzzy was talking to him. We kind of giggled but humored him. We knew it was the cancer and/or the meds.

"Back then, there was no hospice care, but Grandma got a nurse to come from time to time to help her when she needed or when my parents or other relatives could not be there. Nurse Basia. She was such a nice lady. She was already an old woman herself, and she was so caring and full of wisdom. She came here from Greece. She was so good with Gramps. He would do his babble thing, and Basia would answer him. One day I asked her, 'How do you know what he's saying?'

"She said, 'You must listen with only your heart. Your grandpa is in the middle of two dimensions right now. His human side is strong and wants to stay here on earth. His soul, however, is tired and wants to go home; it's pulling him to the other side.'

"Well, that blew my mind, as you could imagine. I told Basia, 'He thinks Muzzy is talking to him.' I laughed, but she gave me a look of such gravity, I froze in my sneakers. Then Basia glanced at Muzzy sitting there on grandpa's bed.

"'Muzzy is talking to him,' she answered me with pursed lips. 'Most animals, especially dogs and cats, have a heightened sense of things. One must never assume they don't know what is going on. I believe Muzzy is communicating with your grandfather—not with a voice, but with his essence or soul. Animals are God's gifts. If we listen close, we can understand everything they tell us. Just because we don't see it or hear it, we can't believe it?'

"Daddy, are you trying to tell me you think Gypsy is talking to you?!" Sarah abruptly cuts into my story.

"Let me finish! Quit barking at me, would ya?"

Gypsy lifts her head again. *"She gets that from you, and she isn't barking; trust me."*

I give Gypsy a look and continue, "One night, I sat with Gramps. He was doing well on this particular evening, a little more coherent than normal. He told me some stories about when he was a boy and how he became a man. Things that made him proud and things that didn't. You know Great-Grandpa was a marine, had a bunch of medals? You know where all that stuff is, don't ya? Put it aside for that grandson of mine."

"Rambling…" Gypsy growls.

"I'm getting to it. This is *my* story, ya know."

"Okay, okay, Martin. Just get on with it, human. Look at her face. I'm sensing fear coming off her."

I observe my daughter sitting so still, not looking directly at me but through me. Fist under her chin, eyes a bit glassy. Gypsy is right.

"Sarah, please don't be scared. You need to trust me."

"Okay, Daddy, I'm listening. Yes, Joey will get those medals."

I take a deep breath. "Well, Great-Gramps told me Muzzy was talking to him, telling him it's a gift that our beloved animals share when they are given the chance to help them transition. I had forgotten about this until very recently. Gypsy came in here about five days ago, and out of the blue I heard her thoughts."

Sarah looks just a bit confused. "Transition? Daddy?"

I roll my eyes. "I'm gonna die Sarah. Gypsy has told me she can communicate with me at my final days to keep me calm and help me not to be afraid."

"Oh, my God, Daddy! Please! I think you're having a stroke!"

"I told you to keep it to yourself. There's that free-will clause again..."

"Sweetie, how can I make you understand…?" Then, an idea hits me. I look at Gypsy. "Give me something to make her see. Help me out here," I plead.

In response, Gypsy proceeds to tell me a little story, and I repeat it word for word.

"Gypsy says this is something only you and she would know. It was right before Joey was born. Hell, now I'm pretty sure it was about nine months before. Your mother and I went on that Alaska cruise, and you were coming by to take care of Gypsy, remember? So, one night you came over alone and you threw up in the kitchen sink. After you pulled yourself together, you ran out to get a pregnancy test. You came back here and took the test; it was positive."

Sarah cocks a nervous smile. "Okay, but everyone basically knows that."

"Yes, we do, but what we didn't know is what you said to Gypsy while waiting for the test results. You were sitting on the bathroom floor, Gypsy by your side, and you were crying. You told Gypsy, 'I hope if I'm pregnant this one goes full term.' Because you'd found out Mike had a chromosome deficiency that was making you miscarry, you went out one night, found someone to have a one-night stand with, and the rest is history."

Sarah leaps from her chair, shaking, turning white.

Gypsy stands up and barks at her. *"Oh, I think she's gonna pass out!"*

"Daddy, I...I...How did you find this out? I...I...don't understand!" she stutters.

"It's all right, sweetie. I'm not mad. I think you could have handled it a better way, but I get it. I'm not angry with you at all."

Sarah takes a few steps back and grabs her water bottle and takes a long pull from it, almost finishing it. After a deep breath, she speaks. "This isn't happening. Daddy, tell me you just knew all along."

I just gaze at my daughter, realizing at the time, the whole world must have been caving in on her.

"Daddy, I'm sorry. It was the only solution, Mike doesn't know Joey's not biologically his, and neither does Joey, and I want to keep it that way."

"Your secret is safe with me, but why didn't you come to me if there was no other solution? I would have helped."

Sarah cries harder. I can tell she's reliving it. "I…we…didn't have the money to go to a fertility clinic. I felt Mike slipping into depression, fearing he knew he was the problem and he wouldn't be able to give me a child. When the one test we did do showed it was not gonna happen with him, well, maybe I went a little out of my mind. This seemed to be the best idea at the time, and luckily it was." She chuckles through a veil of tears.

"Okay…shhhh, Sarah. Calm down, sweetie. Tell me, do you know the real dad at all?"

Her eyes go to the floor as she shakes her head *no*.

"Don't be embarrassed, sweetheart. It's okay, but what if you didn't get pregnant? Were you just gonna keep having one-night stands till you did?"

She throws her hands in the air. "I really didn't think about it, Daddy; please, can we drop it now?!"

"Okay," I whisper. "But this could have gone in a bad direction. Let's just say you were blessed."

Sarah looks at me, her face a tad serene. Gypsy just wags her tail then hides her nose in her paws. "Gypsy says 'Sorry,' but it was the only way to make you see I am in communication with her. So now do you believe us?"

Two big tears well up in Sarah's eyes. "Yes, yes. I don't know how or why, but yes, I believe you."

I observe my daughter as she composes herself, probably trying to wrap her mind around this bizarre yet magical fact. I glance at Gypsy.

"Do I want to know anything else about my other kids while we're on the subject?"

"That would be a no. *Some things are just irrelevant for you to know."*

"Hmmm…good. I can die happy."

"Ignorance is bliss."

"Daddy, why is Gypsy talking to you? Why now?"

"She says it's a gift that is bestowed upon certain animals and their masters. Some humans are sensitive to it, so I guess I'm like my grandfather. I suppose at some point you might want to tell your siblings about this. It may happen to one of you some day. Not sure if it's just the males. Gypsy has no answers to some of these questions—only that it helps us transition into the afterlife."

Sarah's eyes go wide. "So then there definitely is one, a…an afterlife? Heaven? Or a…another dimension?"

"I suppose so. I am not afraid now. This miracle she has given to me, it's like I can see for the first time or hear, just like Nurse Basia told me, with my heart."

I cough. I can't breathe; I'm choking. I feel as though I'm drowning. Congestive heart failure is coming on now. Sarah gets up to hand me a tissue, and Gypsy comes closer to my face and sniffs.

"Your time is closer, Marty. Relax; we are all here. I can show you a vision now."

I sit back in bed. I almost feel light or like I'm half way out of my body, and there right in front of me is my Adele, my wife of over forty years. She beckons to me, and she's smiling. I want to reach out for her, but Gypsy pulls me back in. *"Not yet, lover boy, but in due time. She is waiting, and she will be there to take you as soon as you go."*

Soon, the vision fades and I am staring into Gypsy's amber eyes again.

"Daddy, Daddy…Dad? Hey—you there?"

"Huh? Oh yeah, sweetie Gypsy gave me a…vision. I just saw your mother. She is waiting for me when I go. It's going to be soon, Sarah, very soon." My daughter smiles, her eyes glassy and moist. She is my strongest child.

***

The evening comes again, and I hear my children. All have grown into exceptional adults. They must have cooked. I can hear them having dinner, but I lost my appetite weeks ago. One by one, every few hours, they come in to check on me. I've developed a rattle in my chest now, and even I know it's called the death rattle. Gypsy is right: I'm not long for this world.

Sarah enters my room. "Dad, can you hear me?" I nod with my eyes still closed and hear the patter of paws and then feel my bed gently rock. I open my eyes as Sarah walks over and smiles. She kisses my forehead. "You have my secret, and I'll keep yours until I need to share. We are all here, Daddy, if you need us." She quietly leaves my room, and Gypsy and I are alone again.

"Marty, time is close. I can smell it. Are you feeling okay?"

I nod.

"I really can't explain how this is happening, but all you need to know is you should trust when I tell you we are not alone. I believe humans interpret heaven in many ways. You will understand more when you're there. You will receive an increased level of clarity, and you may remember being there once before. Yours is a perfect human soul to my animal soul. On one occasion as a young pup, I remember how you scooped me up into your arms and I felt safe as I stared into your eyes and you stared back. My soul connected with yours and bonded with it as if I were a human baby. Then I did the same with Adele and the kids. I now had an exceptional pack. My instincts were to protect each of you, and I recognized you as the Alpha. And what an Alpha you were. I have devoted my loyalties to you."

I reach over slowly and scratch at Gypsy's furry chest. She raises her nose up and stretches her skin where I scratch. "Good ol' Gypsy. You are a good dog. Somehow I always knew what you needed."

"That was the connection I have felt since I was a pup. As I matured, you could understand me without speaking. I didn't

understand your words then, either, but read your body language. I can sense when one of you has a bad day. I know when you feel sadness or joy. I knew, long before any of you noticed, when Adele was confused by the illness that deteriorated her mind. I can sense when any in my pack are ill, from the smallest of ailments to big ones. The day you had your heart attack, I had sensed it coming for days, so I'd stayed close to you."

"Yes, I remember. You wouldn't even let me leave the house without you! My God, I couldn't understand why you were being so stubborn that week. You knew, huh?!"

"I knew some kind of bad thing was coming; when exactly, I couldn't be sure. I knew it was going to be life threatening. And when it finally came on, I tried to get you to hear me but you didn't. I knew you would come home again and we would have more time. But now we are at the end of the journey. It's just a matter of time, hours, now.

"Tell me, Gypsy…you showed me Adele. Is everyone I know there? Will I get questions answered?"

Gypsy stands on all four paws, stretches with her rump in the air, then pads in a circle, repositions herself, puts her pretty head on my knee, and lets out a groan. "What's wrong, girl? Don't you have an answer for me?"

She lifts her head again, eyes on mine. *"Adele will be there. Certain other people will be there, important ones in your life, individuals you have made an impact on and maybe some you might not have been kind to. Not all our loved ones may be present over there. They have journeys of their own. I can't say for sure who, what, or why, because everyone's path on earth is different. What I can tell you is this: the purpose of my gift is to calm you so you're not afraid to cross."*

I open my mouth to ask one more question and Gypsy cuts me off. *"No, I don't know anything about alien life or Area 51 or who killed Marilyn Monroe, so don't ask. And I don't know if you will find out once you are there. This is about you, Marty, your journey."*

I laugh. I laugh hard. I haven't laughed this hard in months. It hurts, and I start to cough and choke. Gypsy sits up to give me room until it all subsides.

"Well, how did you know I was going to ask that?"

"I know you, Marty. I know you like the back of my paw. Relax, my human. Your transition is near."

I sigh. "I wish I had more time. That is the only thing that pisses me off. Why do I have to go so soon and leave you all behind? I feel like I have so much more life to live."

"Almost everyone has that request. We never know all the answers, but remember, when you cross over, embrace the enlightened clarity."

The night goes on. I feel more and more like I am drowning, like my body is just shutting itself down. Gypsy snuggles by my side, and my children sit around in the room. I hear them chatting, but I can't join in. They are reminiscing about things like holidays or remembering things they did with Mom, too, and good times with Gypsy.

I hear, "Look, Dad's smiling. Do you think he can hear us?"

And I hear Sarah's answer: "Dad can hear more than you think; trust me."

I start to feel light. It feels as though my soul has disconnected and is just trapped inside a shell. My heart is skipping beats. I hear Gypsy say, "*Let go, Marty. Relax and release from your body. You can be free now.*"

At first it's so hard to let go, but then I see a light and within it, Adele. She's calling to me. I want to go. I glance around to see Gypsy. She barks, and Adele grabs my hand.

***

"Daddy's gone," I say to my younger brother and sister. "He is at rest now." My siblings begin to cry a little.

My brother, Johnny, points to Dad. "He has a little smile on his face." We gaze at Dad and smile, too.

My sister, Samantha, the youngest of us, hugs me tight and whispers, "I hope Mommy was there waiting on him."

I turn my head to them both. "Yes, I believe Mom and Gypsy were calling to him."

"Gypsy?" My brother questions me. "You think Gypsy came for dad, too?"

I nod. "She was always by his side, so she came for him. She made Dad calm and reassured him that it's all right, just like he did for her and Mom when they couldn't go on anymore."

"Oh, I hope that's true. Do you really believe that, Sarah?" my sister asks.

"Yes, I do. Trust me…I do."

The end.

About my Story & Notes.

What if at the last moments of your life, your beloved pet gave you a gift? Though no words are spoken, you hear each other's souls. The effect it has on you is calming to help you cross over without fear or doubt.

What if you were the only one who could hear them, see them? What if they showed you a life past and one waiting in the after, would you think you were hallucinating? Would your family believe you or would they humor you knowing your time is short.

I am part of a little local writers group in my home town. Every now and then we come up with ideas for fun. Part of this group is to keep us motivated in our writing and to help each other write through any blocks we have and, or write ourselves out of a corner.

On one particular day, I suggested I should write a short story, being I never had before and I hoped it jump start my passion for writing. One thing led to another and everyone decided to take the challenge. We decided to write different from what we normally write about and take a step out of our comfort zone, after more discussions we decided to publish them in a compilation joint effort.

This was so much fun to challenge myself that I can't wait to write something else that is out of my norm. I usually write romance, and write from a woman's point of view. This time I wrote from a mans and a dog's. Still in keeping with a magical and or spiritual element I love.

I hope Gypsies gift touches your heart as it has touched my many beta reader's and friends!

About the Author

Robin H. Soprano born and raised in Essex county NJ moved to N. East Florida 25 years ago,

She found her love of writing and published two books. Magical /paranormal Romances, A Soul Mates Promise and Absinthe. Both can be found on Amazon and Barnes & Nobel web sites.

Her love for story telling grows strong and has no doubt she has big angels guiding her creative drive. She says she listens to gut instincts and her strong intuition. She is currently working on some other projects and hopes to get a few more books published. She spends her days enjoying a new life and path she was given. Also, loves reading and watching favorite shows and movies all in the company of her beloved dogs, Corey & Roscoe who make her smile even in her worst days. She currently lives with her boyfriend Harry, who she credits with giving her strength and encouragement in life as well as writing and reads what she's working on. She has a collection of Angels on a shelf in her office she looks to them every day and each has a special word to which helps her do almost anything….

DREAM ~ WISH ~ BELIEVE

Books by Robin H. Soprano

 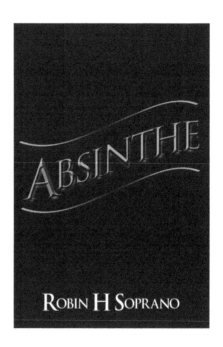

Three Blind Wives (sneak preview)

Saying good bye to people you love hurts.

My two best friends in the whole world are leaving, going separate ways to start new lives. We hug each other tight, huddled into one another with tears. The Fort Lauderdale airport is busy with other travelers scooting by us. We are in their way but don't care. We don't know when we will see each other again and our hearts are breaking.

I've known these girls for only seven years but we all connected right away and have never been apart. I give one last look at Crystal and Dusty. We promise each other with a pact, as soon as they are settled we will pick a place and meet three times a year on each of our birthdays for a girls weekend no matter what.

I leave the airport. I can't stop the tears running from my eyes. I put on my big dark sunglasses. I then head to the parking area and get in my car. As I make my way to the exit, my thoughts are scattered. I still can't believe this is happening. It all started ten months ago, on one of our weekly girl's nights at my house. We poured some wine, put out snacks and Crystal said, "I have a fun idea!" Five little innocent words that changed our lives forever…

Ten months ago….

"It's gonna be all right Renee." Dusty says with her perfect pink smile. "You'll see, I think you and Frank can work this out. He loves you."

"But I don't feel I love him anymore. Just the sight of him makes me tense."

Crystal picks up the bottle of merlot, tops off our glasses and sighs dramatically. "I have to say it Renee. I think you are having postpartum depression…you have knocked out 2 babies in a year and a half. I think you should ask the doctor for some drugs."

"No, I'm fine." I inform my friends. "The separation is good for me right now. It's only been a few weeks and I already feel less tension." I notice they both give each other a look.

"Okay. Fine." Dusty sighs. "Just don't do anything extreme for a while."

"Agreed!" Crystal raises her wine glass. Dusty and Crystal are divorced for good reasons." She spat out, "Our husbands were cheats, liars and pricks. Not Frank. You got a good one there, so if you need time, take it but I'm telling you, he truly loves you and this is killing him."

"Can we please talk about something else?" I urged feeling my temper rise.

"Fine." Crystal huffed. "Listen I have a fun idea. Now just hear me out. It's just for shits and giggles. There is this on-line dating service called 'Blind Date.' I say we sign up and go on some dates. See what's out there."

Dusty looks up from her wine glass, eyes wide, and laughs. "There's nothing out there, and all the guys in our age group want girls in their twenties."

"Oh, I don't know," I answer. "I wouldn't mind sticking my toes in the water, just for fun." I say raising my hand. "I'm not looking for anything but fun."

"Yep, me too." Crystal agreed with me. "We are older, wiser, we know what we want and how we want it. We are independently wealthy and we can take this opportunity into our hands, our rules. Let them buy us drinks and dinner, and then WE decide if we are going to fuck'em and dump'em!"

"So, kind of like we are the guy?" Dusty asks.

We all look at each other nodding our perfectly hair-styled heads.

"Good. Let me show you the web site." Crystal jumps up off my couch and heads to the office where the computer is. A few clicks and we are reading WELCOME TO BLIND DATE.

"This is what I propose we do. We set up one profile for the three of us. It does not require a picture, hence the whole blind date theme. Let's see… Make up a name."

We all quickly lost any previous trains of thought spewing out the obvious stripper names. "Candie? NO!" "Ginger? NO!" "Brittney?"

"No, come on," I say, "We are in our forties. These guys are going to think we're in our twenties with those names."

Crystal points a French painted nail at the screen. "Right here it says age group. 25 to 35, 35 to 45, and then 50 and up. Really?" She huffs, "I'm 48 and I look pretty damn good. What would I want with a 65-year-old? All I see is old balls coming at me!" She shakes her head and makes a vomit sound. "I'm NOT that old yet!"

"Let's lie a little." Dusty offers. "We can fake it. Renee is the youngest of all of us she's 41 so put 35 to 45. I think that's reasonable. And I also think we better hit some yoga and exercise classes at my spa facility. We may need to just tone it up a little. I don't know about you girls but if a man is going to see me naked I want to make sure everything stays in place."

I look at Dusty and Crystal. Yes, they are older than me but are both beautiful. "Not fair. You both have been nipped and tucked, I just do a little Botox here and there and I've had two babies."

Dusty looks up from the computer. "Well Crystal and I let my ex tweak us up before I divorced him. Renee, you're still young. A few rounds in the gym and you'll be fine. You've lost all your baby weight now. Just tone up, plus, the exercise will be good for the stamina. We're gonna need it for the younger guys!"

"What was it like being married to a plastic surgeon?" I ask Dusty. "I would feel he was constantly looking at my imperfections."

"Not Kenny, He was too busy fucking all the franken-barbies he created in his operating room."

"I'm just glad I got my tits done before you hired me to clean his clock." Crystal laughed. "The best part was he hit on me also. Then, you should have seen his face months later when I entered the court room as Dusty's divorce attorney. There I am with my new boobs proving infidelity! He knew he was beat."

We all laugh, "I love some of these stories you two talk about. I wish I knew you guys back then." I say.

"You found us just at the right time." Dusty smiles. "It's when we started to live and have fun."

"I'll drink to that." Crystal raises her wine glass. "I was a nasty bitch when I was married to Greg. The thing that bothered me the most was after I found out he married me for my money. The cheating was one thing because half the time he was drunk and I was told he couldn't get it up most of the time. No, it was the gambling, and lying and losing my money. I don't think Greg Walker worked over a month at any job a day in his life."

I stare at Crystal like she's someone I don't recognize. "I just don't see how someone like you ended up with such a loser like him."

"He was different and younger. Lots of fun. I didn't get married till I was 37. I think I was scared. I worked my life away. Now I'm alone again, no kids. My mother, the merry widow is having more fun than me. She sold the house in Canada and moved to the south of France. I can't wait to go see her."

"Your mom is my idol." Dusty cooed. "But I am happy I have the rehabilitation center for all the ladies recovering from plastic surgery and or reconstructive surgeries. That keeps me busy and I have a wonderful staff helping me."

"Okay girls," Crystal cut in. "Back to the profile. 35 to 45. Check.

"How about the name Anna?" I ask. "It's simple, short, sweet."

The girls look at me and nod in agreement. We put average, curvy body type. Fill in yes to a job but don't mention what. Yes, to a car. Yes, to pets, Dusty has a ranch with horses. Put down just dating, nothing serious about relationships. We hit enter, and within a few minutes we are up on Blind Date.

We start to maneuver around and read men's profiles. Some were funny. Some were very dirty. And then there were a few normal ones.

Crystal was the first to go and text one of them. She keyed, HEY THERE WANT TO CHAT? Soon we all chimed in and found profiles of men that we thought would be fun to chat with and maybe set up a date. We synchronized up the website with our emails so when someone would respond we would know.

About three days in we were flooded with responses. As usual Crystal was the first to chat. His name was Brad. She set up a date on a Thursday night. She told us where and that she would text us if she was in any trouble. If any emergency occurred, we would swoop in for a rescue. The next night we would meet at Dusty's ranch for a girl's night and she would tell us about the date.

***

Friday night we all gathered at the ranch. Sprawling acres with four beautiful horses in magnificent stables. The house was all beautiful brown wood and stone, a Colorado style ranch. She even named it Crooked Pines due to the few pine trees that grew in funky shape.

I pull in her long driveway and park my Mercedes next to Crystals BMW. Before I got to the big front door, Dusty opened it up and let me in. We sat in front of her cave-like fireplace and nestled into her soft smooth brown leather sofas with animal skin throw rugs tossed about.

The place was warm and cozy except for the few deer heads mounted to the walls. Dusty knew how to hunt and loved it. Me? I would turn vegetarian before I shot and killed an animal for food. It's just not in me. I eat meat but I pretend I don't know where it comes from.

Dusty pulled a cork from a bottle of Merlot and poured generously into three wine goblets. Crystal has a smug look on her face. "Wait till you girls hear this."

She raises her eyebrows. "Well, the date was interesting. His name is Mark. He says he is an entrepreneur, of what he was not clear. He says he has his hands in a little bit of everything. To me that means he's broke or out of work and a bull shitter, but he is very handsome and he knows it. I think that's how he gets by. He says he's 45. He's very tan and fit. I met him at the polo club. We had drinks first then we decided to have dinner. He is fun and sexy so that's the only reason I stayed. He thinks my name is Anna of course. After dinner, he walked me to my car and then grabbed me. Put his hand right up my shirt, went for the tits instantly. I was shocked at first, but the kiss was so hot! I felt myself soften into him. I took his bait and rode it. I pressed myself up against him and I could feel him harden. Ladies…he has one hell of a package under his jeans! I think I'll see him again so I can get a better look!"

We laugh and sip wine. "Did you make another date already?" I ask with enthusiasm.

"Oh yes." Crystal replies with a devilish smile. "We are meeting again tomorrow night at the Blue Moon for dinner and then…." She rolls her eyes for dramatic flair.

"So, you're going to sleep with Mark?" asks Dusty.

"I'm not saying yes or no. I'm just saying, it is very possible."

"Go for it." I offer enthusiastically. "I got someone on line too. He wants to meet me. I'm thinking about it."

The girls look at me, their eyes wide with delight. "Really! Let's read his profile." Dusty says grabbing the lap top. A few clicks and we're on.

"Hey the mailbox is full." Crystal points.

"Click on it and see what these guys have to say." I remark with a little sarcasm.

Dusty taps the first one. "This dude is using the name star69. I can only imagine. Let's see what he has to say."

"Hey Anna, hi I want to lick your pussy all night! How about a taste?"

"Holy Shit!" I spat out. "How rude can you get?"

"Okay I deleted him" Dusty said.

"Well what did you expect, he's using the name star69, come on!"

"Next up?" Dusty reads. "Big Daddy" she clicks on the message.

"Howdy Anna. I read your profile. You sound like a fun filly. Come read my profile, maybe you like what you read. Sure would be nice to take you out."

We check out Big Daddy's profile. He's from Texas and lives near here now. He's retired and about 65 years old. Crystal reaches over Dusty's shoulder and hits delete. "No old balls!" She snaps.

"Next." I laugh.

"Hi Anna. You sound sweet. My name is Carlo. Please feel free to check out my profile. Chat with me and see if we click."

Dusty hit the chat button, Carlo was on line.

"Hi there."

We type.

"Hello, how are you?"

"Fine."

"Did you read my profile? What do you think?"

Quickly we search his profile. Carlo. 46, single father of three. Lives in area. Italian and Spanish decent. Born here in the states. Looking for love and a relationship. "Yeah they all say that," Crystal snarls.

"Hi...yes read your profile...would very much like to meet you."

"I'd like to meet him." Dusty said.

Back and forth they went and set up a time and place for next Thursday. Then we clicked over to the guy I was interested in.

"He says his name is Steve. Here it is." I quickly point out.

Dusty reads aloud. "Steve, 48 years old. Single never married, owns his own business, truck driver, originally from Philly. Lives and works in area. Wants to date a nice woman, nothing serious."

"Okay," she says, "Let's see if he's online?"

"He's not on at the moment but let's leave him a message." I offer. "I was chatting with him a little bit last night. I'm not picking up creep factor, but you never know."

"Hello Steve, if you would like to go on a date, message me soon and we will make plans. Anna."

***

Saturday morning, we all met at Dusty's spa facility. Raging Beauty.

We did a Zumba class then a yoga class. We swam and had relaxing massages. One of the attendants brought us some frozen cocktails and we sat in lounge chairs by the pool.

"I heard from Steve." I said. "We are going to meet at the sports pub on main and 1st. Thursday night."

"Good for you Renee. Now remember," Crystal looks at me with her icy blue eyes. "You're separated. Don't do anything crazy you might regret. You should just date. Don't go jumping into bed yet."

"I agree." Dusty lifted her frozen glass.

I took a deep breath and slowly let it out. "Thanks for your concern girls but I wasn't planning on crazy. Just fun. Let's see what happens."

"Trust me," Crystal replies. "Your wounds are fresh and you're vulnerable. Play it safe or else you will just get more confused and hurt. I still wish you would go see your doctor or a therapist."

"I'm fine. Seriously. Let me breathe."

"She's right." Dusty counters. "Nothing wrong with a little breather. Just remember that's all it is. Maybe dating some strange men you'll realize whether you want to stay married or not."

Crystal finishes her drink with a slurp on her straw. "Okay. Friday night. My house, and we tell each about our dates. Do you want red or white wine?"

I toss her a look of derision. "Both" I snort and we all laugh.

A Soul Mates Promise (sneak preview)

CHAPTER 15

Thanksgiving morning, my kitchen is a noisy place. Antonio is in charge of the turkey and stuffing, I'm doing both the sweet-potato and the green-bean casseroles, and Sal is stuffing mushrooms and slicing rolls. And Toby…well, Toby is drooling all over the floor and us.

"Toby, you poor-a thing. The smell of-a the turkey roasting is making him crazy." Antonio makes tsking noises and shakes his head at the dog.

"Don't worry, he will get plenty," I comment, laughing.

Sal throws a piece of cheese to Toby, and he catches it like a pro. "So spoiled," I mutter.

After a while, with not much else to do and everything roasting, baking, or simmering, I go in the next room and turn on the television to watch the Macy's parade. Sal peeks in after a while.

"Do you need anything?"

"No thanks. I'm fine. I just love to watch this parade…kind of a nice, traditional memory from my childhood."

Sal gives me a loving smile. "Best seat is at home. Did you ever go to the parade?"

"Once. My father took us. It was brutally cold, and there were just way too many people. You are right about the best seat being at home on your own couch."

***

I wake to loud voices coming from the kitchen. I open my eyes and try to get my bearings. Glancing at the parade, I realize it's almost time for the big guy in the red suit to make his grand entrance, when I hear Sal and Antonio arguing.

"I couldn't get back. Let it go, Pop. Will you just let it go?"

"Your mother asked for-a you on her death bed. You missed all the last holidays of-a her life."

"ENOUGH, POP! Please!" Sal's pleading at this point.

I get up quickly and bolt into the kitchen. I see Sal and Antonio staring each other down. They look like two angry bulls. Uh-oh. This is not going to be pretty.

"No more, Pop; I can't. Please. I don't want to talk about it."

"YOU COULD HAVE BEEN HERE! NO MORE LIES!"

I can feel my body trembling, but I'm not willing to watch the two men I love most in the world hurt each other.

"What the hell is going on in here?" I demand.

Sal turns away from his father. "He's starting with me about where I was when Mom was sick."

I glance at Antonio, whose eyes are blood red. He also appears to be getting short of breath. I slowly step to his side. "Pop, are you all right? Can you breathe? Sal, get him some water."

Sal brings a glass of water over to his father, but Antonio won't take it. I give Sal a very serious look of disappointment before I take the water glass and hand it to Tony. With shaky hands, Tony takes the glass and sips but won't even glance in my direction.

"I should go, cara. Please forgive me. Holidays are hard."

I step back to get a good look at both of them. "Stop this!" I scolded. "YOU TWO ARE NOT GOING TO FIGHT AND RUIN THIS HOLIDAY! THIS HAS GONE FAR ENOUGH!"

The two of them glare at me in shock. I'm sure neither one has ever heard me yell at anyone.

"Gracie, it's okay. Calm down," Sal says, pain etched into his handsome face.

"NO, SAL. I will not. You have got to tell him where you were and what happened to you. It's time. Right now--or I will!"

Sal knows he is defeated, because I'm standing my ground. I know this will help him…and Antonio.

"What is she talking about, Salvatore? What happened? Where were you? Talk to me, Son."

"Why don't you guys go out to the lanai and talk. Leave Toby in here with me."

As Antonio starts for the door, I turn to Sal and he pulls me into a fierce hug. I feel him trembling, and I understand how hard this is for him.

In a low voice he whispers, "I'm sorry, Gracie. I didn't want it to come out this way. I was going to tell him, I swear I was."

I put my hands on his face and look into his eyes. "I believe that, Sal. But, now's your chance. I think it will help you, and I know he is going to understand. He loves you very much."

Sal follows his dad out to the pool deck.

How does a son tell his father about prison and torture? About the fears. About the long days and nights of wishing he was home with his mother, yet knowing he would probably never see her again…

A few times, I walk by and peek at them. I see Antonio crying; I see Sal furiously wiping his own eyes. I hear them get loud again, but this time it turns into laughter.

When they return to the kitchen, Antonio seems better and Sal seems lighter, as though a huge burden has been lifted. The rest of the day is happy and calm. Maybe now that we all know the truth, now that another ghost is banished, Sal and I are even closer than before.

When we sit down to have our Thanksgiving dinner, Antonio says a prayer of thanks and blessings. I've heard it many times before, but today, underlying the words is a more heart-felt meaning.

I'm so thankful for them both. Sal, by some miracle, survived that prison and found me. Some people say there are no accidents in life. Maybe miracles do happen.

***

I wake up to feather-light kisses on the back of my neck that trail down to my shoulder.

"Wake up, Princess," Sal whispers in muffled tones. "Hey, sleepyhead. Wake up."

I open my eyes and see Sal's handsome, smiling face.

"What's going on? What time is it?"

"It's about five. Sun won't be up for hours, but you were mumbling in your sleep."

"I was? What was I saying?"

Still exploring my body with kisses, his voice is muffled. "If I knew, I would tell you."

"And when I mumble in my sleep you wake me with kisses?"

"Yes," he continues between kisses. "You were starting to panic, and I wanted to wake you up calmly. Is it working?"

"Mm-hmmm."

"Good."

Sal rolls me onto my back and keeps me secure. He kisses my throat, then my breasts, lightly sucking first the left one then the right. I'm about ready to scream with the delightful pain of anticipation. He lets his hand slide down between my legs and slips fingers inside me.

"Sal," I moan, thrusting my hips upward.

"Gracie, you're so warm." His breath on my skin makes me tremble. "I need to be in you--now," he whispers as he thrusts inside and holds me still.

"Don't move," he groans, "I just want to be inside you." His dark eyes focus on mine. "I love you, Gracianna D'Anella."

I just about come undone right then. Lying naked with the man I love buried inside me, his eyes piercing into my soul, using my full, given name to proclaim his love is mind blowing.

"I could stay like this with you forever."

I can't reply. I'm going to come whether he moves or not. Slowly we move, finding our rhythm. He rolls us over, and I'm straddling him, his hands securely on my hips to keep me in place. I am over the cliff. When Sal follows me into ecstasy, an orgasm vibrates me again. I collapse on top of him, panting so hard I can barely speak.

"Is this how you are going to wake me every morning?"

"It's a possibility," he says with a smile as he playfully pats my ass.

I kiss him. "I love you, too, Salvatore Anthony Petroni.". We rest for a while, our bodies still entwined, until my stomach growls. Sal puts his hand on my belly.

"You're hungry, Princess. Let me get your breakfast. What time are you going in to work, today?"

"Around ten," I mutter into my pillow.

***

We go for our morning walk on the beach and find it's a chilly day but beautiful. Sal and I walk hand in hand while Toby searches the beach for treasures.

"Gracie, would you do something for me?"

I stop walking and turn to Sal. He places a hand on each of my arms. "What's wrong?" I ask, searching his face.

"I was thinking about your dreams. On some nights, you mumble and appear to be struggling. Maybe you could go talk to a doctor."

"Doctor?" I echo. "You mean a psychiatrist?"

He nods. "Yeah. You could go see the one I was going to. I'm just concerned about you."

Now I know he doesn't understand. Does he think I'm crazy after all? I look down at our sneakers in the sand. Sal coaxes my chin up with his fingers. "It's just a suggestion, Gracie. Sometimes talking about stuff helps bring it to the surface, and then you can purge it. It helped me. You know that."

"I do know. I just don't know about it for me. Can I think about it? Maybe after the holidays."

"Gracie, do this for me. Sometimes one or two sessions may be all you need. I'll call Doctor Brooks today and see about an appointment."

I gaze into Sal's deep-brown eyes. He looks truly worried, and for that reason alone I tell him to go ahead and make the call. Who knows--it might even help me navigate through this psychic thing I seem to be stuck with.

***

"Holy Mother of God!" I say as I look at the tree in my living room that certainly rivals the one in Rockefeller Center. We had a blast picking it out, and Sal only dropped it twice as we struggled to cut the netting free and maneuver the trunk into the stand.

Sal battles with the lights while I go off to find my ornaments. When we are finished, it really looks beautiful and the smell of fresh fir takes over the room. Pop is worn out by the time we've got the ornaments on, so he leaves Sal and me to finish the last touches. Sal hits the switch, and we are basking in the glow of a million twinkling red, white, and green lights.

"It's beautiful, Sal. I love it. Thank you for this." Sal comes over to my side to get a better look.

"No need to thank me, Gracie. It's ours, together. I love you."

We both take a seat on the couch to admire our work and snuggle. Sal takes my hand. "I called Doctor Brooks for you. They got you in on Monday afternoon at three."

I immediately tense. I know I agreed to go, but I'm not feeling happy about it. Sal gives me a little squeeze. "It'll be fine. Just talk to him"

Feeling nervous, I quickly change the subject.

"You all ready for the benefit tomorrow? Tuxedo and all?"

He smiles big, maybe sensing my apprehension about seeing Doctor Brooks. "Yes, I'm looking forward to a fancy evening with you on my arm."

"Richard will be there, too," I warn him.

"I know," he answers with a smile that reminds me of a cat that's about to eat a canary. "I can't wait."

Absinthe (sneak preview)

CHAPTER THREE

I wake the next morning with my head on my computer desk. I am a little foggy and confused. *Why am I here and not in my bed?* My neck is stiff and my lower back throbs in pain. "What the hell?" I say out loud. I glance around; everything seems normal. The sun is up, brightening the whole room, and I look at the clock. Eleven a.m., Saturday. "Oh, man, I slept way too long…" My eyes dart up to my screen. *What is all this?* I move the mouse up and down, scanning across the characters, then I begin to read. First, I wonder if it is something I left open about the house. Then, I read, and read some more. I realize I am the one who apparently tapped on the computer keys and wrote these paragraphs, but I don't remember doing it at all…

My name is Prudence Henriod Ravensdale. I was born in France in 1777. I came to America in 1798. I had to leave to save myself from the danger that had darkened my sister's life and mine. When I arrived here, I was just twenty-one years of age. I didn't bring much with me. Only the money given to me as payment from an evil man named Marcellis Dubied. He had wanted the recipe for the elixir we made to help heal the sick. It was our secret, and we did not want to divulge our recipe to him or any other. Only the purest of hearts and family bloodline can understand it. He threatened to reveal us as witches. I am a healer, but many fear what they do not understand. Monsieur Dubied even murdered our friend, a doctor, to frighten us, to get us to sell him our recipe...Oh, how I miss our friend, Dr. Ordinaire.

My sister, Jonet, was forced into a marriage to the nephew of M. Dubied. After I fled my homeland, I was never to see my sister again. M. Dubied had wanted us to use our gifts for profit by marketing our healing elixir, but we never gave him the proper recipe. In the end, we were forced out of fear to sell it to him, but we had ommitted a particular healing herb. M. Dubied, some time later, discovered our deception. In the meantime, he had partnered with a winemaker, Louis Pernod. Together, they opened distilleries to produce the elixir, even though it was without the secret ingredient, and named it absinthe. The green liquid became popular, even more so than any of the fine wines in France. As a result, Dubied and Pernod made their fortunes from my family's treasured recipe.

Some years after my arrival in America, I met a wonderful Englishman by the name of Bernard Ravensdale. Soon after our marriage, he moved me south to New Orleans so I could be close to people who spoke my native tongue. We built this house and were blessed with three healthy children. Life became even better when I found Lisette. Half Haitian, half French, she knew many of the healing ways, as I did. Her grandmother, a very strong voodoo queen around these parts, had taught her well. I took her in as an au pair, and together we made our healing powders and elixirs. She went to church with us and cared for my children as if they were her own. Because she was pure light of heart, I shared my family's secret recipe with Lisette, and she was able to make our special green elixir as well as I could.

Much too soon, the darkness of my past followed me here and loomed around us, threatening once again…

I realize I am sitting so still, almost frozen in my chair but taking deep breaths. I don't know how long it took to write those short, completely unfamiliar paragraphs, or how long I was knocked out, or how the words appeared here. But here it sits, all lit up on my computer. *Did I do this? Did Prudence write this? How?*

I search online for the next several hours, trying to find any information at all about the people mentioned in the mysterious writing. Some of the names come up, but there is not much on the Henriod sisters. It would seem that recorded history scrambled it up. I decide that the next thing on my list today will be to go to City Hall to gather information about the house itself. Then, I'll try to contact any living descendants to see what other information I can get.

After a hot shower and some strong coffee, I go to sit out in my garden courtyard, trying to wrap my head around what happened last night. I remember going through the box and the notebook, then the toast I made to the house… "I drank the Absinthe!" I say very loud to no one but the flowers and trees that are scattered across my back yard. "No way…" I shake my head. "Could it have…?" I remember Jack's story about this stuff causing hallucinations. *Holy shit!* I freak out for a minute or two, then I quickly try to calm down. I realize I feel fine—more than fine, actually. But, along with that feeling of wellness, I am somehow picking up an emotion of desperation and an odd sense that my help is needed by Prudence Ravensdale.

I get in my car and head out to City Hall. During the entire drive over there, I am on my cell phone with Helen, the realtor who sold me the house. The first words out of her mouth when I ask her some questions are, "Oh, shit! Please don't tell me the house is haunted!"

"No, no, no...not at all!" I assure her. "I just want to research the history of the house. I found some things behind a wall removed during some renovations." I couldn't tell her that maybe I was the one being haunted in some mysterious way. I wanted information, and I couldn't sound like a complete freak.

"Oh, whew!" She laughs. "Let me see what I can retrieve for you, and I'll get back to you ASAP!"

I thank her and pull into the parking lot. I enter City Hall and ask where the hall of records would be. The clerk shows me to the correct area, and I immediately get to work. I am thrilled to find several pieces of information.

I find out my house was built in 1803 for Mr. and Mrs. B. Ravensdale.

By 1810, there were 3 children, all girls, born to the Ravensdales: Suzette, Juliette, and Andrea.

Mr. Ravensdale was a businessman who came from England. But, here the trail runs cold; there is nothing else. I look up death records, next:

Mrs. Prudence Ravensdale:

Born the 23rd day of October 1777 in Pontarlier, France. Deceased the 10th day of November 1821 at 44 years of age; cause of death unknown. Survived by husband and three children.

"Death unknown? And where did you all go?" I whisper. I continue to look up anything I can about any Ravensdales in the area, but I find nothing more of consequence. Just a quick blurb in a local paper of the time. It stated that Prudence's eldest daughter, Suzette, had gone to the University of Cambridge in England. Upon seeing this, I wonder if the whole family started over after their mother died. Maybe their father took them back to his home because he had lost his wife.

I am deep in thought when the vibration of my cell phone startles me. I reach into the pocket of my jeans and pull out my cell. I'm happy to see it is Helen.

"Hello, Helen. I'm in the hall of records right now, and I found some stuff, but not much. The trail seems to just go cold after Mrs. Ravensdale's death."

"Yes, I didn't find much myself, either, so I made a phone call to a Sebastian Charles Devonshire. His name is the one we have on documents for your house. He is from the U.K. but has dual citizenship. He travels back and forth for business. I had to leave a message with his secretary, so I left your name and number. I hope that was all right?"

"Yes, that's fine. Thank you, Helen. I hope this Sebastian can help me out. He sounds important." I chuckle. "What type of business is he in?"

"I believe he is some kind of CEO or something like that," she replies.

The first thing that comes to my mind is that Mr. Devonshire is probably too busy to talk with me and I might have to get pushy, but I don't care. I need to know the history of my house and of the Ravensdales. I also feel the pull of creativity beckoning. I am obviously sitting on my next book, one that is being told to me, I'm beginning to believe, by what must be the spirit of Prudence Ravensdale. But, what I don't know is why, and I'm still wrapping my head around the how. Before I can even try to write her story, I need more facts. I have too many loose ends. I arrive home exhausted, my mind racing in too many directions and suffering from sleeping at my computer desk all night. I need a nap. I plop down on my sofa and drift into a sound sleep.

***

Across the country, Sebastian C. Devonshire is in a board meeting in his company's New York City office. At thirty-eight, he has already been the head of his family's business for a few years. When his father died, Sebastian had inherited big shoes to fill, but the leadership transition had gone smoothly. With today's meeting finally over, he gathers his things, strides from the office building, and climbs into his waiting limo. As he leans into the comfortable leather seat, his secretary phones to inform him that a Sharie Donovan, who bought the family manor in Louisiana, desperately wants to speak with him.

"I wonder what she could possibly want?"

"Well, sir, she apparently wants some information on the house. It seems there were some items found."

"Items? What kind of items?"

"I'm not sure. All I was told is that she is a writer and wants to know more about the house and its history."

"All right. Thank you, Janice. Please give me her contact information, and I'll try to reach her directly."

"Yes, sir. I'll get that to you right away."

His curiosity aroused, Sebastian googles Sharie Donovan after pouring himself a martini and settling in for the evening at his Fifth Avenue penthouse. "Well, what do have here, Ms. Donavan? Romance and mysteries are your passions, are they?" He sips the martini, the smooth liquor warming his throat. Sharie's big, brown eyes, sincere and friendly, gaze back at him from one of the photos Sebastian happens across. Reading her bio, he detects a sense of humor and adventure. With some free time coming soon, he thinks about taking a trip down south, playing a few rounds of golf, maybe going fishing and paying Miss Donavan a visit. He realizes he hasn't been to the manor since he was a small boy. His mother is the one who stopped wanting to vacation there; she just wanted to be rid of the place. *We haven't been since Father passed,* he remembers. He relaxes back into his leather chair and proceeds to make travel arrangements on the phone. He then emails Miss Donovan:

From: Sebastian C. Devonshire

To: Sharie Donovan

Dear Miss Donovan,

I hope this email finds you well and you are enjoying your new home. I received a message that you are inquiring about the manor and its history. I understand there were some items found. If you would be so kind as to share with me what it is you found and what information you seek, I will do my best to answer your questions.

Sincerely,

S.C. Devonshire

Lightning Source UK Ltd.
Milton Keynes UK
UKHW020617070922
408466UK00006B/40

9 781935 795490